AFRICA IS GOOD 2

A Collection of Stories About The African Market Woman & The African School

Written By:
Lawrence Nyong &
Obi Chidebelu-Eze

Illustrated By:
David Newborne

AFRICA IS GOOD 2

A Collection of Stories About The African Market Woman & The African School

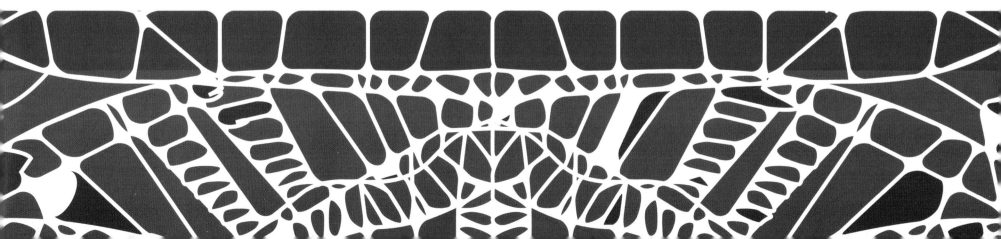

Library of Congress Catalog Card Number:
TXu1-675-543 The African Market Woman
TXu1-675-547 The African School
Washington D.C.
February 26, 2010

Information:
Dove Publishing, Inc.
P.O.Box 310326
Atlanta, GA 31131

Tel: 678.612.2749
Web: www.dovepub.com

Africa Is Good
902 South Randall Road, Suite C230
Saint Charles, IL 60174

Tel: 630.452-0163
Web: www.africaisgood.com

Layout and jacket design by Josh Murtha

PRINTED IN SOUTH KOREA.

DEDICATIONS

From Lawrence Nyong

This book is dedicated to all the children around the world, especially those in developing countries. I want you to know that your parents, your nation and the circumstances of your birth were given to you by God as a gift! No matter what your family background, color, or nationality, you can go anywhere from anywhere. Just decide where you want to go and build up the courage to reach your destination. God is no respecter of persons. History proves that a boy whose father was raised in a distant Kenyan village can become the President of the most powerful country in the world and that a young woman's act of kindness could place her in the family tree of the Savior of the world. The choice is yours!

Also, I want to dedicate this book to my grandfather, Etubom Oku Etim Nyong, who used the virtue of love to elevate his family and the entire community. Although he is gone, he is still my example; I am who I am because of him.

Finally, I dedicate this book to my loving, beautiful, vivacious wife, Faith and my children—Lawrence (Essien), Lauren (Abassi-oku), and Victor (Efiong). You all inspire me to fulfill my primary purpose as a loving husband, a devoted father and a leader in society; to you I am forever grateful.

From Obi Chidebelu-Eze

This book is dedicated to my wonderful wife, Mia. Please accept my love and thanks for all that you do to make our family balanced and strong. Above all, thanks for your love and for your devotion to myself and our children.

Also, I dedicate this book to my children—Jonathan (Chukwunonso) and Jordyn (Amarachi). You are both the seeds of leadership for the future. You are the investment of my youth, and with the Creator's direction the ones who will invest in making a better, brighter and beneficial tomorrow.

Finally, this book is dedicated to all of the children on the African continent and the rest of the world. I humbly request that you all strive, not only to make Africa good, but also the entire world.

REVIEWS

It's been my honor and privilege to have known and observed Lawrence Nyong for the last twenty years. Focused, consistent, diligent, industrious, ingenious, entrepreneurial and altruistic are some words that rightly describe Lawrence. I recommend "Africa is Good" to all who admire such qualities. Lawrence's qualities are readily observable in the writing of "Africa is Good."

Carlton Arthurs
Statesman, Belize Central America

The future of Africa lies in the hands of young Africans. Africa is Good and continues to get better. We Africans must love Africa and work for the betterment of Africa and Africa will yield its fruits... I support the efforts of putting Africa in a good light. Africa is Good!!!

Ezekiel Guti, Ph.D.
Founder & President Zaoga International
Zimbabwe

'Africa is Good' is a wonderful book about the daily life style of the cultures of Africa. This is an enlightening resource for guiding students through everyday situations in the continent of Africa.

Andrea Fuse Brooks
Commissioner Sumter County Georgia
Retired Educator

Africa is Good is an exceptional title for an exceptional book! In our current society and the large numbers of broken families it is refreshing to learn the pro-family culture and values of Africa. Africa is indeed good. The book is an excellent educational tool as it inspires and encourages personal and cultural growth.

Roselyn Daniels
Thirty five year Educator/Reading Consultant
Atlanta, Georgia

COMMENTARY

By His Eminence, Edidem Ekpo Okon Abasi Otu V

This work though not written in Chapters provides an insight into the creative capabilities and the unbounded energies of our people which has remained pristine to date. Specifically, the African Market Woman story delves into a social-economic system erected substantially on the agility of individual initiative, available choices and free competitive markets.

The imageries depicting the practice of having a livelihood as an imperative for survival and the obligation of satisfying compelling needs are laced with a wealth of secondary allusion to some veritable portions in the Bible. This is no novelty. It is to assist the reader to comprehend and appreciate the dynamic relationship between being hospitable, meticulous and focused on the one hand and the relevance of peaceful co-existence, diplomacy and the accomplishment of something of importance at all times on the other.

It is my hope and expectation that reflections presented in the African Market Woman story will induce a larger number of persons to participate more constructively and intelligently in the strive to attain lofty heights without blemish as well as succeed as a people and a nation.

His Eminence,
Edidem Ekpo Okon Abasi Otu V,
Obong (King) of Calabar &
Grand Patriarch of Efik Eburutu Kingdom
Calabar - Nigeria

FORWARD

By Former Ambassador, Andrew Young

What is it about the great continent of Africa that fascinates and interests us? Why is it that the continent and its countries have been misunderstood and taken out of context? Africa has issues and problems like everywhere else. However, in Africa's case, the negative reports offered by the media have greatly outweighed any positive news. Yes, Africa has poverty-stricken areas, high incidence of AIDS outbreaks, scathing reports of government corruption, and so on. However, Africa's current condition did not occur overnight. For centuries former colonial empires have occupied and plundered the continent, various regimes have done nothing towards good governance or the betterment of the people, some citizens and non-citizens of the continent's sovereign states only sought to exploit, take and never give back, etc. However, this is not the time to blame; it's the time to build.

I can understand why the authors of this wonderful book felt it important to convey the message that Africa is good. So, what does it mean to say that Africa is good? Well, the Bible says that God Almighty, after creating the world and all that it entails declared, "It is good." No matter how neglected, overlooked and almost blacklisted the continent of Africa has become, the declaration of God still stands, "Africa is good."

I have had the privilege of working with many global leaders on many African projects. I know the continent inside out. Lawrence and Obi have taken on a worthwhile challenge; the challenge of educating young Africans and the rest of the world about the good of Africa. This book is announcing what I believe is soon going to be known to the rest of the world. I want to echo their sentiments, Africa is good!

These well-written stories give Africa a personality, while putting flesh on issues. They will enable you to compare African life with your own as you connect to the characters with both head and heart. The foundational lessons of each story will help guide young people to become future champions, ensuring that Africa is good and that it stays good. The themes you will encounter as you read are:

- Africa is good because it demonstrates the joy of marriage and celebrates it as the core foundation of a great family life.
- Africa is good because it shares how family lives in the collective community and that it truly takes a village to raise a child.
- Africa is good because it reminds us that every child deserves an education. An education guarantees the expansion of the horizons of possibility which improves the village…the town…the city…the state…the country…the continent and ultimately the world.
- Africa is good because it shows us how business is interlocked and interdependent on the land and other businesses while supporting the family and the village.

I want to congratulate Lawrence and Obi and ask you, the reader, to support them in their life-changing mission, Africa is good!

Andrew Young
Former Ambassador, United Nations
Chairman GoodWorks International, LLC

TABLE OF CONTENTS

AFRICA IS GOOD 2

A Collection of Stories About The African Market Woman & The African School

THE AFRICAN MARKET WOMAN

EARLY TO RISE

It was an unusually hot morning in Calabar, a beautiful coastal city in the southern region of Nigeria. The air was already filled with the sounds of cars and buses and the clattering of breakfast pots and pans. If you listened closely, you could even hear the sounds of houseboys' and mama's singing as they swept their porches and yards with brushes made from palm fronds.

As usual, Mrs. Gloria Ekong had already started her day early, before the rooster crowed. Mrs. Ekong was a hard working woman who made a modest living selling her wares at the local market. Today was Ambo market day and Mrs. Ekong had vegetables and fruits to sell. The day before, she had been to her little ten acre farm to help her husband, Eno-Obong Ekong, harvest some of the items she wanted to sell: okra, tomatoes, green leafy vegetables, red and green peppers, onions, bananas, plantains, papayas, and oranges.

Algeria

THE MONEY BELT

After getting dressed, Mrs. Ekong put on her money belt. The money belt was the most important item she would need as she went about her business of selling at the market place. The money belt was not really a belt to hold up her clothing, but a piece of cloth that went around her waist and secured the money she made.

Shortly, after she put on her money belt, the rooster crowed and Mrs. Ekong knew from tradition that it was about 6:15 am. She heard several knock knock sounds and opened the door to find her nephew and niece, Okon and Nkoyo, respectively. Her sister, Margaret, was leaving her children with Gloria as she had an important meeting that Saturday in the city of Enugu, a few hours away.

"Well children, are you ready to come with me and learn about the market?" said Mrs. Gloria Ekong.
"Yes, mama," replied the kids.
Then Okon said, "You know Aunty Gloria, we love to learn and we are very excited about going with you to the market."
"I am delighted to hear it," replied Gloria as she ushered them to the breakfast table. After enjoying a quick breakfast of bean cakes, eggs, sweet bread and orange juice, everyone got into Gloria's car and headed for the Ambo market.

Angola

GETTING TO MARKET

The Ambo Market where Gloria, Okon and Nkoyo were heading, was about a 45 minutes drive from their home in Calabar. As they made their journey, Gloria pointed out the famous palace of the Obong (King) of Calabar. "In fact," she informed the awestruck children, "Obong Ekpe Bassey is a second cousin of my husband Eno-Obong. I've met him on a few occasions during some of the annual festive celebrations."

"I wish I could fly on a plane," said Nkoyo wistfully as they passed the Calabar International Airport.
"I'm sure one day, with a lot of hard work, you will. But today, we are going to the market to learn how to make money."
"So I know I'll be able to afford the ticket!" exclaimed Okon.
"You certainly will be able to learn several things today, and this is just the beginning of your education in commerce," replied Gloria.
"Commerce, what's commerce?" asked Nkoyo.
"Commerce is the art and action of making money by selling goods or services," said Aunty Gloria. "I am so glad you asked this question and you are both excited to learn. I will do my best to answer all of your additional questions, and keep you excited about business."

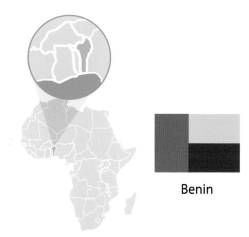

Benin

BUSY LIKE A BEE

The market was busy. When Mrs. Gloria Ekong and the children arrived, there were many men and women opening up their shop stalls at the market place. Many were off-loading the items they brought to sell, while others were sweeping and cleaning their shops. The market had its own smell. Sometimes, depending on where you were, it smelled like fruit and fresh vegetables. At other times, you could smell livestock like chickens, pigs and cows. The strongest smell, however, came from the women who sold food. During breakfast it smelled of fried eggs, fried yam, akara a fried black-eyed pea fritter and akamu or ogi which is a tangy corn custard.

Just like the smells of the market place, the colors were just as exciting. There were beautifully dressed people in their colorful African attire; orange and yellow, brown and green, purple and royal blue. There were the rich colors of the market stalls and the vibrant reds, yellows, oranges and greens of the produce. All of these things add life to the market and made it a wonderful place to be. And everywhere, vendors harping, buyers haggling, and traffic passing.

"This place is great," thought Okon as he and Nkoyo helped their aunty carry some of the fruits and vegetables to their shop. The siblings were both amazed at how busy everyone seemed, but happily observed that no one was too busy to call out greetings and inquire about the welfare of those to whom they were talking.

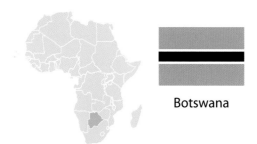

Botswana

THE NEXT DOOR

Fortunately, Mrs. Ekong's shop was not too far back in the market. They soon arrived at shop number 333 and heard someone say, "Good morning Mrs. Ekong." It was Mrs. Mary Archibong whose market shop was beside Mrs. Ekong's in number 334.

"Good Morning, Mrs. Archibong," replied Mrs. Ekong.

"Good morning, Mrs. Archibong," Okon and Nkoyo chorused.

"Well who are these pleasant and well mannered kids?" asked Mrs. Archibong.

"These are my sister's children, Okon and Nkoyo. They will be my young apprentices for the day."

"Oh how wonderful," exclaimed Mrs. Archibong. I am certain you will learn and observe a lot of great things here at the market."

Burkina Faso

SETTING-UP THE PRESENTATION
ARTISTIC ARRANGEMENT

"Put those things toward the back of the shop," Aunty Ekong directed as they returned from their third trip to the car. They slumped into some seats at the back of the shop to rest. As the children caught their breath, Mrs. Ekong began washing and arranging her fruits and vegetables in neat rows on trays at the front of the shop. "Why do you arrange the fruits and vegetables?" asked Nkoyo.

"Fruits and vegetables are perishable produce that, when harvested from the ground, have soil and insects on them, and so must be washed. Also, things that are arranged always seem pleasant to the eye and this attracts customers. In business, you must find ways to stand out or show your goods, so people will find them attractive and want to buy them. Would you like to try arranging Nkoyo?"

"Yes, I would mama." Nkoyo carefully and artfully arranged tomatoes, peppers and onions into stacks of three or four on top of each other. Having observed the ladies, Okon began arranging the fruits. He stacked the papayas and oranges in groups of four just as they had done with the vegetables. There were so many different varieties of fruits and vegetables like mangoes, almonds, tangerines, pineapples, papaya, guava, coconuts, cashew, green leafy vegetables, bitter leaf, red pepper, okra and so much more. Aunt Gloria had to place them in baskets all around the shop. The bananas and plantains, which were in bunches, were cut into smaller bunches and placed in different spots around the floor of the shop on raffia mats. These raffia mats were made in the same way baskets were made by weaving palm fronds in a grid like pattern. By the time the trio finished setting up, it was about 9 o'clock in the morning and the market had officially opened.

Burundi

THE FIRST KNOT IN THE MONEY BELT & BREAKING EVEN

It was not long before a woman walked into the shop. Mrs. Gloria Ekong gave her a warm greeting of welcome. The woman had a baby strapped on her back with a cloth similar to the brown tie-dye outfit she was wearing. The baby was sleeping peacefully on her back and was not disturbed by any of the market noises and sounds. Since it is the custom, because refrigeration is not always available and because of taste, the woman was shopping for fresh ingredients to prepare okra soup for the evening meal.

After browsing, handling and inspecting the vegetables closely, she finally asked, "How much are your tomatoes, onions, peppers and okra?"

"The tomatoes are three naira for half a dozen, the onions are two for one naira, the peppers and okra are both twenty each for two naira," replied Mrs. Ekong.

"Please give me two dozen tomatoes, ten onions, twenty peppers and forty okra pods. How much is that all together?"

"That will be twelve naira for the tomatoes, five naira for the onions, two naira and four for the peppers and okra respectively. The grand total comes to twenty-three naira," responded Mrs. Ekong having worked out the math in her head. The woman paid and commented, "Your vegetables are very fresh and I like your prices. I will be back." The happy mother left the shop with both hands filled with waterproof bags.

Cameroon

THE AFRICAN MARKET WOMAN

"That was nice to hear the lady say she will be back," said Nkoyo.

"Yes, it was nice to hear," replied Mrs. Ekong. "It means our produce is appealing and priced well. Hopefully, she will tell others about her bargain at our shop and others will come too."

"Aunty, I noticed you do something interesting." Immediately, after that lady left, you placed twenty naira in the cloth around your waist and tied it into a knot."

"Okon, you are a sharp and observant boy," affirmed Mrs. Ekong. "Yes, I did do that. As we were arranging the items in the store, I made a quick calculation of what it costs your uncle and me to produce these fruits and vegetables. I realized I needed twenty naira to recover the starting costs, and the amount of what we had spent to begin with. I tied off the money in my belt to show I had accomplished my first goal."

"In business," she continued, "one of your first goals should be to recover the money you started the business with. This is called breaking even. After you have broken even, the rest of the money you make is called a profit. When your business, is profitable, it means that it consistently earns you extra money. You want to keep such a business going. Sometimes it takes quite a while for a business to offer a profit. However, it is wise to think about not continuing if your business is unprofitable for a long time."

"Wow that is very interesting aunty. We have both learned something else while working with you at the market," said Nkoyo.

"I'm so glad to hear it. Continue to keep watching and staying **focused** as you will see the benefits one day," Mrs. Ekong encouraged.

Cape Verde

GOOD CUSTOMER SERVICE

Another customer came into the shop. He was interested in buying some bananas and plantains to go with the peanuts and yams he had bought from Mrs. Archibong. "Hello Madam," he addressed Mrs. Ekong.

"Hello Mr. Essien. It has been a long time since you came by my shop. Have you been well?"

"Thanks for asking, I've been sick with malaria, but I am doing much better now. I came to buy some bananas and plantains. My daughter, Akwa, is about to celebrate her sixth birthday and she loves plantains. She told me she wants to eat plantains every day next week. I need enough to make her happy. As for me, I like bananas and really enjoy them with peanuts as well as rice. What are your prices?"

"It is fifteen naira for the plantain on the large stalk and two naira for each of the small bunches. The bananas are usually twelve naira for the large stalk. However, since you are one of my favorite customers, I will sell them to you for ten naira. The small banana bunches are one naira each."

"Okay Madam Ekong, please give me three stalks of plantain, and one stalk and two bunches of bananas. If I did my calculations correctly, this should come to a total of fifty seven naira."

"Yes, that is correct," replied Mrs. Ekong collecting the money from Mr. Essien.

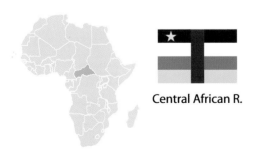

Central African R.

"I can't carry all these plantains and bananas, so I will take what I can carry and return for the rest." Mrs. Ekong put the banana bunches into a bag. Mr. Essien carried them with one stalk of bananas. After a few minutes, he returned and carried off the two stalks of plantains. Mr. Essien smiled happily as he said goodbye to everyone.

"Aunty Gloria, it appears that what you do for a living makes everyone happy. First, the woman with her baby and now Mr. Essien," expressed Nkoyo.

"Yes, my work can be very rewarding when people are happy and satisfied," agreed Mrs. Ekong.

Chad

THE SECOND KNOT & MAKING A PROFIT

"Aunty, you have done it again!" Okon commented excitedly.

"What have I done again Okon?" inquired Mrs. Ekong with a twinkle in her eye.

"You have tied another knot in your money belt," said the young boy.

"Yes, yes, I did do that shortly after Mr. Essien left the shop the first time to take the bananas to his car. I have netted a profit." The children danced jubilantly around the shop. "Does this mean we are rich and can now go for the day?" asked Nkoyo.

"Oh not at all my precious ones; we just got here and have only seen two customers. We are going to see a lot more people. We are going to sell more food stuff, fruits and vegetables and learn more about the importance of this money belt to a market woman such as myself," replied Mrs. Gloria Ekong prudently.

Throughout the day, the children helped their aunty rearrange the fruits and vegetables as customers walked in and out of the shop. At one point Okon grumbled to his sister, "It seems more customers are asking questions about the freshness of the items than are actually buying them."

Congo

THE THIRD KNOT & PERSONAL EXPENSES HOUSEHOLD NEEDS

After lunch, the pace of things really picked up at the shop. Since Mr. Essien left, they had managed to sell most of the vegetables. Mrs. Ekong was pleased she would not have to carry home a lot of perishables.

All of a sudden, Nkoyo started leaping for joy. She nudged Okon while pointing to Aunty Gloria's money belt. To their amazement, a third knot had now appeared. "We've made a profit." "We can go home rich!"

"I am excited that you are excited about making money and doing business," laughed Mrs. Ekong. I will use my profit from this third knot, to take care of my personal expenses." Anticipating, Nkoyo's question, she elaborated, "Expenses are things like the boarding school fees we help pay for your sibling, Eteka, and your cousins Ekanem, Effiong, Kingsley, and Charles. Mr. Ekong pays these expenses from the profit from our farm. I use my profit to pay for expenses that keep our house going like gas, water and electricity. I also pay for everyday items like toiletries and food. I have already included my shop's rent in the amount set aside from the first knot when I broke even on my business expenses. Whenever I can, however, I **barter** with Mrs. Archibong to save money and avoid letting my wares spoil and go to waste."

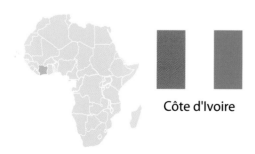

Côte d'Ivoire

TRADING WITHOUT MONEY

"What does barter mean and how do you do it with, Mrs. Archibong?" Nkoyo asked curiously.

"Mrs. Archibong could you come here for a moment?" Mrs. Ekong shouted so her neighbor could hear.

"Yes, how can I help you Mrs. Ekong?"

"Mrs. Archibong, can I barter with you for ten bars of Ivory soap and two big boxes of Omo washing detergent?"

"Just a minute. Yes, you may," replied Mrs. Archibong as she hurried back to her shop. She returned with the requested items and began looking around Mrs. Ekong's shop.

"The Omo boxes are ten naira each and the soap is one naira each coming to a ten naira total. The grand total is thirty naira. Please give me some okra, oranges and plantains." With a nod from his Aunty, Okon hurried to gather these. When he set them down, she deftly gathered thirty naira worth of the freshest.

"Now, Nkoyo, please double check that these items add up to thirty naira," directed Aunty Ekong winking to Mrs. Archibong over the young girl's head. Nkoyo calculated and energetically affirmed, "They do mama."
"Mrs. Ekong, you have such wonderful help. It's always a pleasure doing business with you, but today was particularly delightful," she said smiling. Thank you for helping us barter, children," she waved goodbye as she returned to her shop.

"She didn't give us any money," exclaimed Nkoyo.

"That's because she gave Aunty the washing detergent and soap as an even exchange. Isn't that right, Aunt Gloria?"

"That's right, Okon. Bartering is exchanging goods and services without paying for them with money," replied Mrs. Ekong.

Djibouti

TEACHING OTHERS

The day continued at the shop with several people coming in to buy fruits and vegetables. At one point, two of the children's friends, Daraima and Edidiong, came into the shop with their mother. The kids shook hands, hugged and spoke excitedly to one another. "What are you doing here in this shop?" Daraima asked Okon.

"We're spending the day with our Aunty Gloria in her shop," replied Okon.

"Edidiong, it has been a very busy and exciting day here at the shop and we have learned so much about business," said Nkoyo.

"You have? Well, tell us what you've learned."

"We have learned how to arrange fruits and vegetables so they look appealing to customers."

"We've learned about breaking even, making a profit and paying expenses," replied Okon.

"Also, we have learned how to treat customers such as yourselves and your mother so you'll want to come back," replied Nkoyo.

"And how to barter!"

"Wow, that's a lot of stuff," expressed Daraima. "But, I don't even know what it all means," replied Edidoing.

"I know we don't have much longer in the shop as mama is paying your aunty, but maybe we can all talk about it on the school playground on Monday," urged Daraima.

"Absolutely, Nyoko and I will share all we know. Who knows, maybe there will be others who will be interested in learning about business."

Egypt

CLEANING UP & CLOSING DOWN

Shortly after their friends left, the kids heard their aunty say, "It's time to clean up and close the shop. Nkoyo please get the broom and sweep the entire shop for me. Okon take down the stacks of oranges, tomatoes, pepper and onions that were not sold and place them in the bags we used to bring them into the shop earlier this morning."

While the children did this, Mrs. Gloria Ekong put the bananas and plantains back on her cart, made a quick trip to the van, returned, and took the last load of only plantains to the van. Nkoyo had finished sweeping and joined Okon with his bagging. Mrs. Gloria Ekong then loaded the vegetables and fruits the children had bagged.

Equatorial Guinea

THE FOURTH KNOT, GOOD HELPERS & THE REWARD

"Okon and Nkoyo, you have both done a wonderful job sweeping the floors and bagging the produce. I'm very impressed and really delighted that you worked with me today at the shop. In fact, I am so impressed with your hard work and eagerness to learn that I am going to reward both of you," expressed Mrs. Gloria Ekong. "Hard work in business or in school always deserves a reward. A reward gives you something to look forward to and a reason to work towards something."

She loosened the fourth knot that was now on her money belt and took out ten naira. "Here is five naira for you Nkoyo and here is another five for you Okon."

"Thank you, Aunty Gloria!" exclaimed both children while jumping up and down. The kids were very happy and thanked their aunty as they took the money.
"In case you were wondering children, my money belt now has four tied off knots. I took money out of the fourth knot to reward you both. The fourth knot in the money belt is also money from profits just like the second and third knots. However, this money is money that I spend on things I want such as fixing my hair, shopping for a dress or shoes, buying a gift for a friend, giving money to the poor and needy, and rewarding hard working nieces and nephews for helping me at the store," the trio laughed.

Eritrea

"We have learned so much at your shop aunty. We can't wait to come back and be your helpers," declared Nkoyo.
"In fact Aunty, on Monday we will be sharing with Daraima and Edidiong all we've learned from our experience at your shop."
"Wow, I am so impressed. Not only are you two great apprentices," encouraged Mrs. Ekong, "but you have already started making plans to be teachers. That is excellent."

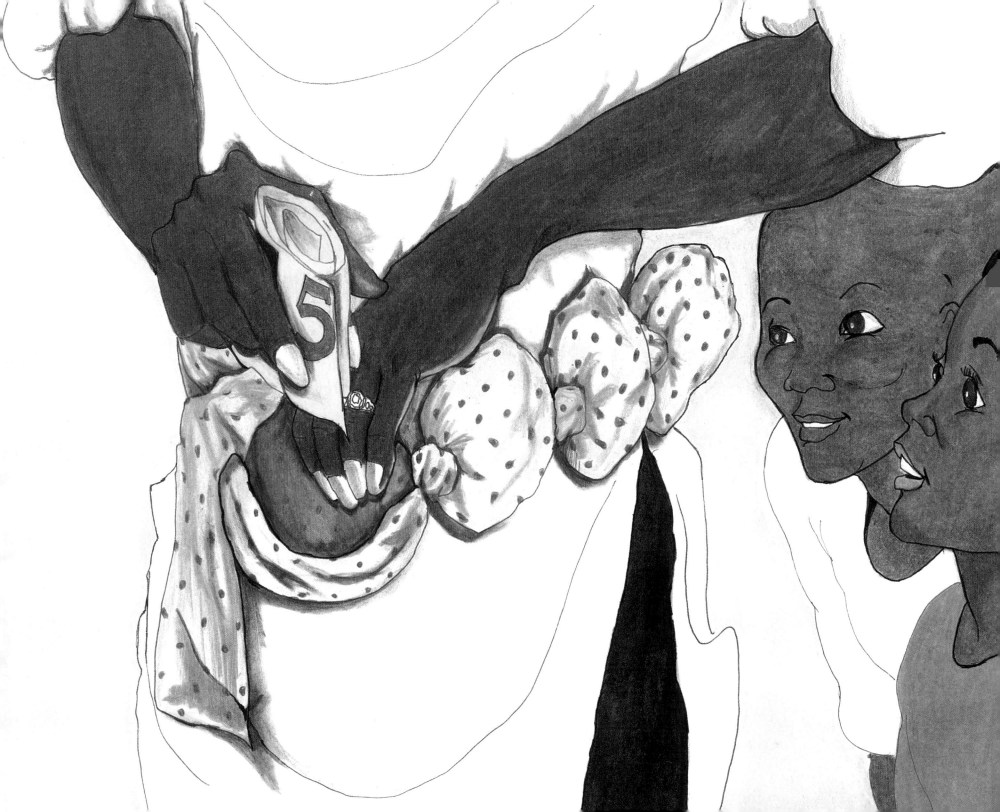

HARD WORK ALWAYS PAYS OFF

As they walked out of the shop, they saw that a few shopkeepers had not yet closed, others were sweeping, counting money, or arranging unsold items.

Okon and Nkoyo had a new found respect for people who ran shops at the market place and an even greater respect for their Aunt. As far as they were concerned, she was one of the hardest working people they knew.

Okon and Nkoyo stopped at a candy shop. They carefully thought about how much of their well deserved reward they would spend and decided to spend only fifty kobo each. They would show their parents the remaining four naira and fifty kobo and put it in their respective saving jars at home.

Ethiopia

REFLECTION & REST

Mrs. Gloria Ekong was impressed her niece and nephew had not spent all their money and told them so. She knew her sister would be pleased as well, "I can see you've really learned something. It is always wise to put aside money for a rainy day and it is also wise to give about ten percent to a worthy cause or to people in need."

"Thank you, Aunty Gloria. We had a great day." Mrs. Ekong was glad, especially since she'd had the privilege and opportunity to teach them about running a profitable business.

During the drive home, the sights Okon and his sister had seen earlier faded and darkness gradually took over. The children observed street vendors who sold their wares and carried them on their heads along with little lanterns. They sold delicious food, beverages, or household and personal cleaning items. He couldn't wait to tell his parents what he had learned. Nkoyo was in a deep sleep. The music of her snoring filled the air of the car. A few miles before reaching their destination, she was jarred awake when the car hit a bump in the road.

Gabon

THE FIFTH KNOT & DOING IMPORTANT THINGS OF INTEREST

"Did you know you were talking in your sleep?" Aunty Gloria asked Nkoyo.

"I was snoring," Nkoyo responded surprised.

"Yes, you were and you said something about a fifth knot," teased her brother.

"Is there anything like a fifth knot, Aunty Gloria?"

"You know, Nkoyo, I have never tied off a fifth knot. However, as you were sleeping, it occurred to me that I should be setting aside money not only for leisure, but to build and fund other things I am interested in. I am very interested in funding and starting a school in my village of Creek Town. So thank you Nkoyo for saying that in your sleep and Okon thank you for remembering it to inspire the idea. It appears we sometimes learn even while we are sleeping."

"You are welcome, Aunty Gloria, even though we don't know how we helped. It seems everybody learned something today," replied Okon.
When the van pulled into Mrs. Ekong's driveway, Okon and Nkoyo's mum ran out to greet them. "How was your day?" she said while hugging and kissing her children.

Ghana

"We had a great day. We learned so much at Aunty Gloria's shop and we can't wait to tell you all about it."
Mrs. Ekong then asked her sister, Margaret Iniabasi, about her journey to Enugu. "It was a good business trip. It was even better because I had enough spare time to make a visit to Federal Government College to see, Okon and Nkoyo's older brother, Eteka. He was excited to see me and shared so much about his first weeks. Gloria thanks for taking the kids today on such short notice. I am delighted they've learned so much."
"It was my pleasure, Margaret. Every child really needs a hands-on approach to learning business. After all, business is a very important part of life and the **resources** from work **fund** virtually everything we do. I'm looking forward to having my little apprentices join me on a regular basis.

Guinea-Bissau

THE AFRICAN SCHOOL

WALKING BACK FROM SCHOOL

The school bell had just sounded, as Okon Bassey and his classmates dashed to get their bags to go home. Some of the 600 students at St. Silas Primary School had bicycles, but most students had to walk to school. Okon, who was now in primary six, and had been walking the three miles to school for about a full semester. As a result, walking now seemed such a breeze. His daily trek started because his bike needed a new back tire. Okon was torn between fixing the tire, and saving for the national common entrance examination fees. His father, Dr. James Bassey, had made it all too clear to him that saving for his education was priority over everything else. As his father put it, "Whatever you get easily and without effort you, end up not valuing as much." Hence, he was forced to save for his exam, as was the Bassey family custom.

Guinea

A STUDY PLAN

On his way home, a voice shouted "Okon, Okon wait for me so we can walk together." The voice belonged to Rotimi Johnson, one of Okon's neighbors. "Have you started studying for the big exam?" "Yes, I have been reading a little, but I need to come up with a study plan," replied Okon. The two friends continued talking about how they would prepare for the upcoming entrance examination to secondary school. Both boys shared the great ambition of attending one of the best secondary schools in the country. They decided to study and review every day for two hours minimum. Rotimi was very good in math and science while Okon was good in English, social studies, and literature; each agreed to coach the other in their respective areas of strength.

When Okon arrived home, his mother told him one of her good friends, Mrs. Musa, who lived up north in Kaduna, had invited him for a visit during the long summer holiday. Okon was very happy and excited about the prospect of traveling to Kaduna to visit a woman he regarded as his aunt. He realized that the trip would afford him an opportunity to visit Federal Government College Kaduna. This school was his first choice of the secondary schools he desired to attend because he wanted to live in another part of the country. Furthermore, this school had over the years nurtured leaders in the area of business, and business was a subject that Okon loved to study.

Kenya

NATIONAL COMMON ENTRANCE EXAMINATION (NCEE)

The weeks came and went, and the NCEE date drew nearer. Okon and Rotimi religiously kept to their daily two hour minimum study schedule. They had pledged to do this without neglecting their daily family responsibilities which included: sweeping, washing dishes, and taking care of their younger brothers and sisters. Now, two days before Okon would write the exam, he kept the midnight oil burning and his mother worried about how little Okon had slept over the past few days. "Okon you need your rest. I don't want you staying up late anymore!" Okon obeyed his mother, and reverted back to his two hours study regime.

At last, the anticipated day arrived. Okon awoke very early to do his daily chores. He was in the middle of sweeping the kitchen floor when his mother grabbed his hand and began to pray, "Dear God, thank you for giving me a wonderful son, Okon. I'm very grateful for all you've done for me and Okon. Please help Okon do well on his examination today. Help him remember all the information he has studied, and give him supernatural wisdom to answer the questions correctly. We ask all these requests in your Son's name, Amen."

"I love you son. Just do your best; that's all your father and I ask for." Just as she said this, Rotimi's mother honked her horn. Okon hurriedly kissed his mother, ran to the car and waved as Mrs. Johnson drove away.

Lesotho

SCHOOL VISITS AND INTERVIEWS

After the exams, life returned to normal for Okon, his neighbor Rotimi and all the primary six students heading to secondary school. The end of the school year was one week away, and Okon was very much looking forward to his upcoming visit to Kaduna the following Friday. As she left for work that morning, his mother informed him, "I'll stop by the post office on the way home to check for your much anticipated plane ticket from Aunt Musa."

Okon was out playing and keeping a watchful eye for the return of his mum when he heard her call, "Okon, Okon! You have mail from Aunt Musa." "Oh yes, this must be my air ticket," he shouted jubilantly. Okon tore open the envelope and was surprised to find a prospective (invitation to visit) letter from Federal Government College Kaduna in addition to his ticket. Things were all coming together for Okon who was scheduled to travel to Kaduna in just two weeks.

Liberia

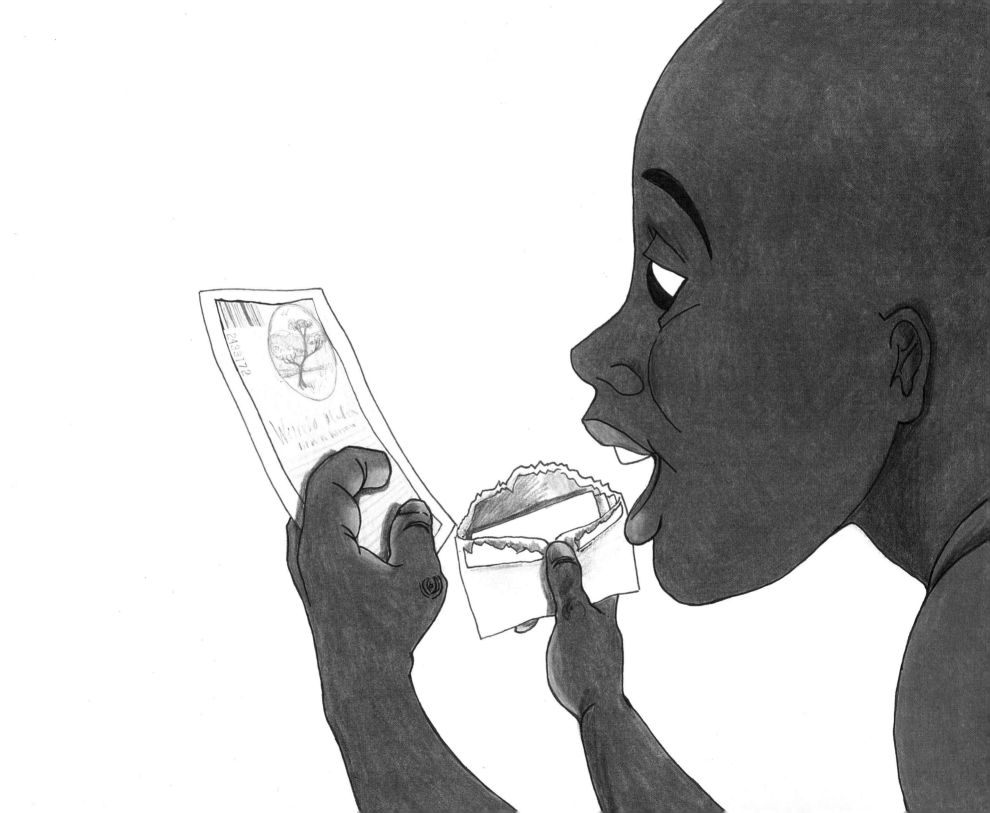

THE AFRICAN SCHOOL

The two weeks went by quickly and Okon headed eagerly to the airport for his first plane flight ever. "Okon make sure you listen to your aunt and follow her instructions," charged Mrs. Bassey. "Also, remember what we've always taught you: add value to your visit. Ensure your aunt misses you when you leave because you've helped her in sweeping the house, washing her cars and doing whatever may need to be done," his mother called after him as he prepared to board for the two and a half hours flight from Calabar to Kaduna.

Libya

Okon could not wait to buckle his seatbelt. He was both a little scared and wildly excited when the plane became air-borne. "Good afternoon ladies and gentlemen, this is your pilot, Captain Obianyor," he heard over the intercom. "On behalf of Okada Airlines, I would like to thank you for flying with us to Kaduna. We will be flying at an altitude of thirty six thousand feet, and should be arriving Kaduna in about two hours and fifteen minutes. Please sit back, relax and enjoy your flight."

Okon was disappointed. "What happened to the extra 15 minutes?" he wondered. However, he relaxed as instructed and reveled in his first flight. Too soon, the experience was over and the plane touched down in Kaduna.

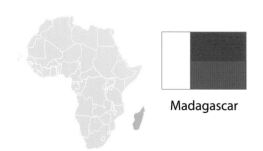

Madagascar

TOUCH DOWN

Mrs. Musa was waiting at the airport anticipating the arrival of Flight 212 from Calabar. She did not have to wait long before Okon's plane landed and taxied down the runway. The plane reached the gate and Okon quickly rushed out to meet his aunty. Mrs. Musa wore a beautiful, velvet colored outfit traditionally worn by the Hausa people with a white scarf to protect her face from the cold harmattan. She hated these cold conditions. In fact, during previous Harmattan seasons, she had suffered feverish symptoms and catarrh, and she did not want a repeat of it this year. The Harmattan is a dry and dusty West African trade wind. It blows cool air south from Sahara into the Gulf of Guinea in the winter between the end of November and the middle of March.

Okon and his aunty hugged warmly as he chattered excitedly about his first plan trip. "Why did the flight only take two hours and fifteen minutes rather than the two and a half scheduled?" he asked with boyish curiosity. "I don't know. I guess pilots can speed just like drivers on the road," said Mrs. Musa directing him from the baggage area to the airport terminal entrance exit where her driver was keeping a keen eye out for the pair. Adepoju noticed his employer from a distance and pulled up alongside them. He welcomed Okon with a handshake as he loaded his few bags in the trunk and then drove them the short fifteen minute ride to Mrs. Musa's home.

Malawi

INTERVIEWING WITH THE BEST

Okon greeted his uncle, a very wealthy man who made his living by trading minerals, and his two cousins, Dauda Bata and Amina, with hugs, well wishes and presents from home. Even though Okon was not a blood relative to Dauda Bata and Amina they were like his real brother and sister. Duada Bata was just one year younger and Amina almost two years older than Okon. The trio had known each other since birth when they all lived in Calabar. However, Mr. Musa's relatives wanted him to return home to the north and he had returned with his family about a year earlier—though it seemed longer to Okon. The children had numerous questions to ask one another so the chatter continued throughout the evening and the duration of Okon's relatively short visit.

A couple of days after Okon's arrival, his aunty Mrs. Musa made an appointment for Okon to interview at Federal Government College (FGC) Kaduna, his first choice pick of schools in the nation. He was looking forward to visiting his prospective new school. However, the morning of Okon's appointment, Mrs. Margaret Bassey called from Calabar with Okon's NCEE results. Because Okon had performed very well, he had already been accepted into Federal Government College (FGC) Enugu, his second choice pick on the forms he had filled out. Okon was a little disappointed as he really wanted to stay with his aunty and attend Federal Government College Kaduna. "Don't worry. You did very well on your exam and I'm very proud of you," said his mother. "Then why didn't I get into my first choice?' Okon asked in frustration. "Well it may be because there are a desired number of students that are selected from each region of the country, and FGC Kaduna has filled their quota of students from southeastern Nigeria." Mrs. Musa, who was determined to at least show her visitors the campus still insisted on taking Okon to meet with the Headmaster, Mr. Kunle Coker.

Mali

TRY YOUR BEST AND DON'T GIVE UP

Adepoju drove Okon and his aunt on a campus tour of the administrative building, classrooms, dormitories, and athletic center. Okon was impressed with the school and wanted to meet with Mr. Coker to see if he could convince him to over-rule the quota system, and accept him into his school.

"Come in please," beckoned the headmaster's secretary, Mrs. Uchechukwu. "Good afternoon, my name is Mrs. Musa and this is my nephew Okon. We have an appointment to see Mr. Coker." "Please have a seat and he will be with you shortly," Mrs. Uchechukwu said. "Good afternoon Mrs. Musa" said Mr. Coker walking into the room a few minutes later. "Who is this quiet and handsome young man with you?" the headmaster asked. "I am Okon Bassey and I'm Mrs. Musa's nephew. Can I tell you that I am so impressed with your school, and the way it is run? FGC Kaduna is absolutely amazing, and I would be honored to be one of your students this school year." "Thank you Okon for the kind remarks regarding our school." Mr. Coker went on to say, "It is unfortunate that I do not make decisions as to which school students get assigned. There is a governing body in the Federal Ministry of Education that evaluates each student and decides which school will best suit them. I was recently made to understand that you have been given admission to Federal Government College Enugu. Please, allow me to tell you that it is a very fine school."

Mauritania

SCHOOL STARTS

The interview was disappointing and brief, but Okon had tried his best. Now he struggled to reconcile himself to the fact that he had no say in the matter. In two weeks, school would start for all Federal Government Colleges in Nigeria. Okon returned to Calabar to prepare for school; shopping for the school supplies and uniforms required by FGC Enugu.

The day before his departure, Mrs. Bassey took Okon to their pastor for prayer. Pastor Sunday Adeboye prayed for Okon, and advised him to, "Be determined and pursue excellence in everything you do." Also, he encouraged, "Strive to be a leader and to make positive efforts in the right direction with your studies."

Morocco

THE FIRST DAY OF BOARDING SCHOOL

It was a hot Thursday morning in September when Okon carefully packed all the required supplies from the information packet provided by his new school. The list included the following: five white short sleeved shirts, two long sleeved shirts, five sky blue shirts, five ox blood shorts, five dark brown shorts, seven white colored undergarments, three bed sheets and matching pillow cases, one bucket, one jerry can, eating utensils, plates, two brown Clark sandals, five dark colored socks, five white socks, a pair of tennis shoes, two black belts, a mathematical set, one book bag with ten note-books, five number two pencils, five black or blue pens, an eraser, one iron, two bath towels, two sets of pajamas, one machete, one hoe and a box of provisions with popcorn, noodles, sugar, tea, soap etc.

Enugu was the state capital of the former Anambra State and was about three to four hours driving distance from Calabar. Mr. Victor Inyang, Okon's uncle came to take him to school and to give him some fatherly advice. Okon's father, Dr. James Bassey had traveled out of the country to speak at a very important medical conference in which he was a speaker. Okon's uncle was definitely filling in, and had driven his brand new Peugeot through the night from Lagos in order to arrive very early in the morning. "Are we ready to hit the road?" he asked as he exchanged hugs and kisses with his sister and her family. "It's around 6AM. If we hurry, we should be able to get out of town before traffic starts to build up and it becomes impossible to drive." Realizing her brother was correct, Mrs. Bassey hurriedly assisted them in packing the boot, and then they were on their way.

Mozambique

ARE WE THERE YET

"Uncle, what time will we get there?" Okon asked as they drove away. "We should be getting into Enugu around ten o'clock in the morning, and to your new school about thirty minutes later."

On the way, Okon's uncle Mr. Inyang advised Okon, "Be obedient to your teachers and seniors. Make the family proud." To reinforce his point, he offered an African proverb: "A poor man's yam never gets burnt." "What does this proverb mean?" queried Okon. "A rich man has many yams," Uncle Inyang explained, "so he can afford to play around while his yams are in the fire. If any of his yams get burnt, he simply gets more yams to replace them. On the other hand, a poor man has only one yam. That's why he is forced to watch it with care while it roasts in the fire." Okon's uncle continued and said, "Your parents love you and your siblings very much. We were all brought up to look after our children, and to treat each child as the only and most important child: just like the poor man's yam." Okon nodded and quipped, "I am a yam."

Uncle Inyang laughed, "Yes, but you know, the yams don't only mean children. They represent a number of things in life like school, friends, work, and visions for the future, etc. Okon, I would like to share with you some of these lessons from my upbringing, so you don't burn your future yams." Through the course of the car trip, Okon's uncle and mother enumerated on the following yams: "Take care of yourself, love God, keep your family first, honor the family name, be kind to people, and be courageous." They rounded off by saying, "God bless you my son; don't bring shame to the family name. Now go and make us proud in school."

Namibia

A GOODBYE TEAR

The car was now approaching Independent Layout and Okon could see the fence of his new boarding school. The car turned the corner and quickly approached the school's amazingly large, eye-catching main entrance of two hands interlocking to form an arch. The sign at the school's gate read, "Welcome to Federal Government College Enugu. Our Motto is Unity and Peace." Okon exclaimed, "Wow, this is so impressive!"

Niger

THE AFRICAN SCHOOL

Okon's uncle drove along a meandering driveway that traversed the beautiful campus. At the administration building, all new students were welcomed and assigned to their respective dormitories. There were five dormitories in the school, Peace, Liberty, Unity, Honesty, and Independence House. "If you had a bird's eye view," one of the Orientation staff informed them, "you'd see they form the shape of a cross."

Okon came back to the car park to tell his mother and uncle, "I have been assigned to the first floor of Peace house." They drove to his dormitory, helped Okon unpack his belongings, and arranged his room in an orderly manner. Around four, Uncle Inyang announced to his sister, "It's time to head back to Calabar." Mrs. Bassey hugged Okon and whispered a parting blessing in his ear as she climbed into the car. Okon waved and cried as the navy blue 504 Peugeot drove out of the car park. It was a happy and bittersweet day for the family.

Nigeria

ON YOUR OWN

Okon Bassey was now on his own to think and successfully plan both his academic and social life. He stayed in his room to read the school handbook and daily time table for all students. From this information, Okon discovered there was a mandatory meeting for all new boarding house students at seven o'clock that evening in the dining hall. About fifteen minutes before the meeting, Okon began to find his way there. Along the way, Okon met a fellow Class One student, Jide Nzelibe. Jide was an unusual student in that he was born in the United States. Although Jide's mother was an American, his parents wanted him to get a Nigerian education, and to learn his father's Ibo culture.

Okon realized there were students from many different tribes, ethnic groups, socio-economic backgrounds, and geographic locations. Okon understood the ranking system and realized that, as an entry level student, he was also a class one student.

Republic of Congo

THE MEETING

In the dining hall, students were organized in ranks from class one all the way to class six. The meeting opened when the senior school prefect, also called the Head Boy, welcomed all the new students. In response to Jide's quizzical look, Okon explained, "Being the Head Boy is an honor and privilege conferred by the Head Master."

The head boy proceeded to introduce his deputies by name and role. There were prefects for both the young men and for the young ladies. He first introduced the assistant senior prefect, the labor prefect, all three house prefects for sports, dining hall, social and then all the senior students. The senior students were very easy to identify because the boys wore trousers, and the girls wore skirts with a blouse; while the rest of the male students wore shorts and the females wore dresses. The prefects were responsible for managing their various areas, and were respected because of the authority they had been given.

Okon became concerned when he heard the head boy say, "All class four students you must respect class five students, class three students you must respect class four students, class two students must respect class three students, class one students must respect class two students, and class one students the cutlass and buckets will respect you." Okon was quickly learning that students had power and rank like the military. He would later learn that this respect for the students in the classes above was part of character building and aided in cultivating respect for others, especially those more senior. After the meeting, Okon went back to his room, and continued to read the student handbook as he had been instructed by the senior prefect. The most important subject in the handbook was the different daily time schedules to be followed by all students. Each class level had unique timetables and responsibilities which ensured that FGC: Enugu ran like a well oiled machine.

Rwanda

THE AFRICAN SCHOOL

5:00AM - Wake-up
5:30AM - Morning Jog
6:15AM - Morning Duties
6:45AM - Bath Time
7:00AM - Morning Inspection
7:30AM - Breakfast
8:00AM - First Class (Academics Period till 2:30PM)
2:30PM - Lunch Time
3:30PM - Afternoon Nap Time
4:15PM - Afternoon Prep.
5:00PM - Sports or Manual Labor
6:00PM - Bath
6:30PM - Dinner
7:00PM - Evening Prep (on Monday, Tuesday, Wednesday, Thursday, Sunday)
9:00PM - Prep Time Over
9:30PM - Lights Out (for class one to three students)
10:30PM - Lights Out the Entire School (except during exam period)

Senegal

STAYING FOCUSED

After reading the entire student handbook, Okon became very serious and anxious. He realized he would have to be very organized in order to keep up with the daily school schedule. Moreover, he wanted to excel in his school work especially since his mother was not there to remind him of the things he needed to do. Okon Bassey was now twelve years old and completely on his own.

The ages of other entry level students ranged from eleven to thirteen. He was in a different state, and the city of Enugu was about four hours away from his hometown of Calabar. He would have to keep his part of the room clean, his bed made every morning before inspection, his shirts and shorts pressed, and his sandals polished. In addition, Okon would have to ensure that he stayed organized and on top of his school work.

Seychelles

LIGHTS OUT

The school bell sounded for lights out, and Okon put on the brand new pajamas and robe his mother had bought him. He quickly set his wrist watch to sound at five o'clock so he could take a few minutes to pray before their morning jog. He went to the washroom to brush his teeth. Upon returning to his room he knelt by his bed, said a quick prayer, and then climbed under the covers for the night.

Sierra Leone

Somalia

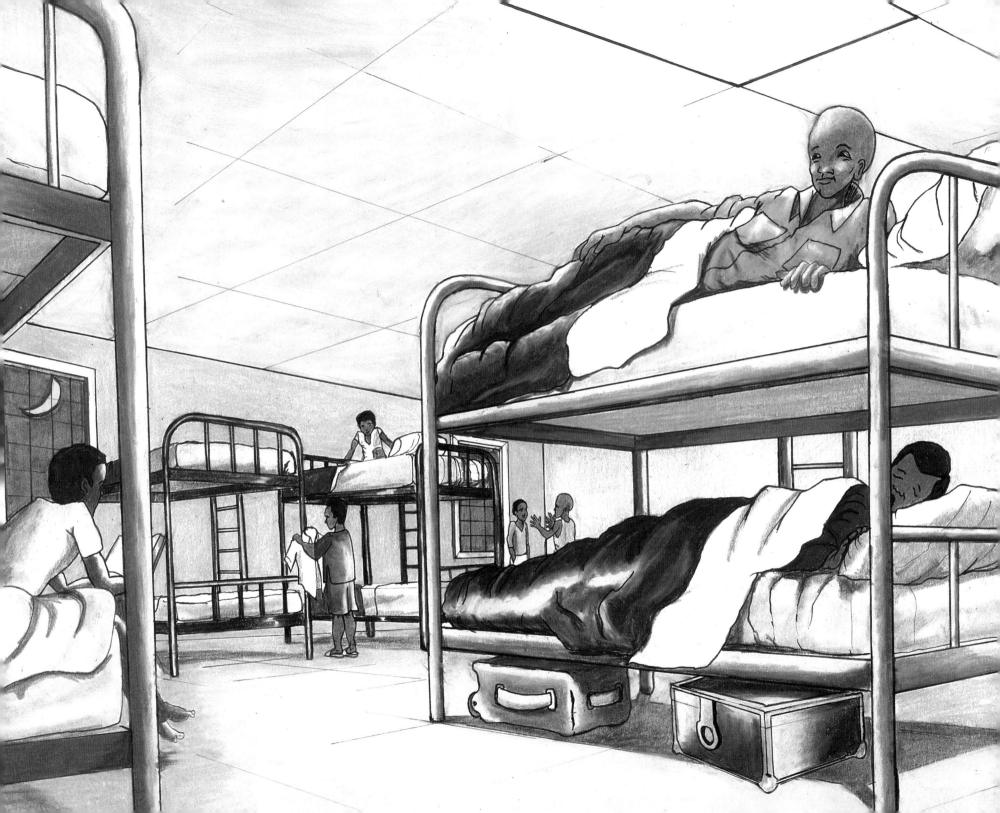

Many things about boarding school were interesting and new for Okon. For instance, when he was younger, he and his sister Nkoyo had shared a room. As they grew, and the family became better off financially, they had moved to a bigger house and he'd been given his own room. Now, here at school, he found himself sharing a room with nine other 11 to 13 year old boys. Also, he had found it difficult making friends in his dorm, but realized that just like him, many of the entry level students were in shock over their first day's experience. Other than Jide, who lived in Honesty House, he hadn't really met anyone that day. He was sure he'd soon make a friend in the dorm, but wished he'd had one right now.

At 9:25, the bell sounded. Five minutes later, the lights went out in the dormitories where class one, two, and three students resided. Okon could hear the faint sounds of one or two kids crying in his dorm room. He knew they were homesick. He was too, but he knew he had to be strong. Okon longed for his family, and knew no one was allowed to visit except on visiting Sundays. He had four weekends to wait as visiting Sundays were every last Sunday of the month. Just then he said a silent prayer of thanks that he hadn't been accepted into FGC: Kaduna which was further away and not as convenient for his family to visit. He pledged to be patient, stay focused, and make his family proud.

South Africa

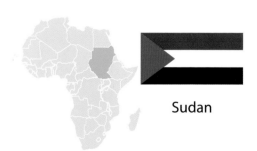

Sudan

THE WAKE-UP CALL

The wake-up bell sounded and all the class one students lined up in pairs for a two-mile jog. The first day of jogging sounded like mass chaos as most of the students were crying about the drastic changes in their lifestyle. Because it was a Monday, Okon was eagerly looking forward to the first assembly that was going to take place. He rushed from the dining hall to the assembly where the rest of the students were gathering to hear the principal. Some students had met the principal during their entrance interview, but Okon had received an automatic letter of acceptance.

Mr. Uzoho the Headmaster was a calm man, but rumors had already been floating around that the Assistant Headmaster Mr. Tunde Bakere was not so mild mannered. Apparently, Mr. Bakere did not tolerate nonsense and getting into trouble with him was to be avoided at all costs. Okon was eager to hear the headmaster and his staff so he could form his own opinions.

Swaziland

Tanzania

MONDAY MORNING SCHOOL ASSEMBLY

The headmaster welcomed the new boarding students as well as the students regarded as 'day students' who went home daily after school. He then introduced his staff and made a few remarks about his expectations for the school, the students and his staff. Okon was happy because he liked the headmaster's comments, and he had made a couple of friends that morning.

The Gambia

Togo

THE AFRICAN SCHOOL

The bell rang for the first period of academics to begin and the students hurried to get to their respective classes within five minutes. Okon was assigned to class one 'E' which was the last room in the class one building block. During class, his homeroom teacher explained, "Each day has six periods with a long break for thirty minutes, and a short break for ten." There was so much information to take in thought Okon. However, the news that really captured his attention was when his teacher explained, "Out of the thirty five students in this class, one will emerge as the best and come first. Coming first in class means that when all the subjects taken are graded and added up, he or she has obtained the highest score. It is customary," he continued, "for all exam results to be posted in the administration building for all to see." Okon immediately flashed back to his uncle's admonition in the car, "Okon do not shame us; do your best. Make us proud." Okon Bassey came to understand that the grading system created an environment of fierce competition among the students. After all, nobody wants to be at the bottom of anything, particularly when that data will be publicized.

Tunisia

Uganda

WHAT'S IN YOU WILL HELP YOU

Okon Bassey's entire upbringing would inevitably pay off. His family had laid a good foundation emphasizing self discipline, academic excellence, and a positive work ethic. Okon was poised. He had made up his mind to shine like a star, and excel beyond anyone's expectations including his own. "The fight is on and the game begins," Okon declared to himself as he collected his book from his school locker to take back to the dormitory. Little did Okon know these words would ring true as he would have to fight to stay on top of every grade and class post, as well as the game of life itself! Thankfully, he was up to the challenge. It was going to be a productive as well as an amazing year.

Zambia

Zimbabwe

ADDITIONAL LESSONS

Principles

The African Market Woman was written to foster and nurture the concept of the entrepreneurial spirit for our youth. This story models and illustrates several important lessons. From the list below, choose 3 principles and explain what you have learned about them from the characters in the story.

- It is important to put forth your best effort.
  - o Organize your wares so they are attractive to customers or present your work so it is desirable to your teachers/parents.
  - o Good customer service is important in attracting customers; just as friendliness is important in keeping friends.
- Plan ahead or prepare in advance for your day, work, education and future.
  - o A wise person budgets for expenses, luxuries, necessities and the future.
- After you have worked hard and done your work well, relax and enjoy yourself.
- A good relationship, even with your competition, can be of mutual benefit.
- It is important to take care of others in your community.

Early To Rise

It is a well known African fact that going early to bed means early to rise. The Individual with purpose and direction rises early and plans ahead. We must live our lives on purpose; stay on task and work hard. This is important in both business and life itself. As usual, Mrs. Gloria Ekong had already started her day early before the roaster crowed. In addition, she went to her farm to harvest what she needed to sell a day before going to the market. Strive to plan ahead and set goals for life.

The Money Belt

Instead of a cash register, market vendors store their funds in a money belt. In this story, the money belt and the subsequent tying off was the symbolic reminder that certain financial goals have been reached. Managing your money flow and keeping some in savings are essential core value practices in business. Oftentimes, money and making it is the singular goal or reason for being in business. However, having a good name in business is a benefit that should be sought after and desired. Hence, it is important to ensure that you are in business for the right reasons, including providing a good service to your customers.

ADDITIONAL LESSONS

Getting To Market

Success in business takes a lot of hard work and requires more than a positive attitude. Yes, Mrs. Gloria Ekong could have stayed at home and could even have sold her wares at her house. However, she went to the market where more people could conveniently find what she sold. Moreover, she had to partner with her husband to grow the crops they sold as well as collect them in advance so she would be ready for market day. In many cases, dear reader, things don't just come our way without significant effort on our part. In the event that opportunity refuses to knock, we have to work hard and create opportunities for ourselves.

Busy Like a Bee

Mrs. Gloria Ekong, and others who sold at the market, worked diligently to set up shop and organize what they sold. Plan carefully in business and not in haste.

The Competition Next Door

Competition is a normal and even healthy thing in business. Competition should cause you to improve your service, skills and product. Competition should not cause jealousy or envy. Rather, it should allow admiration of your competitor's uniqueness that generates a desire for you to improve your own business. Mrs. Ekong and Mrs. Archibong were able to mutually benefit from each other's businesses by bartering wares the other didn't supply.

Setting-up the Presentation

Mrs. Gloria Ekong, and others who sold at market, worked diligently to set up shop and organize what they sold. This not only enabled them to keep track of their inventory and to keep fresh supplies available to customers, it also made it easier for customers to locate what they needed. Not to mention the fact that an attractive display might entice customers to purchase more than they had originally intended.

The First Knot in the Money Belt & Breaking Even

Breaking even is a very important principle of business. A business that cannot break even will close. A worker's appetite works for him, for his hunger urges him on. This statement reinforces the idea that trying to break even, and make a profit is vital and critical. Hunger is a concern and a basic requirement. When you are hungry for something, it is not pleasant and forces you to take action to satisfy it. Hence, hunger can be a friend if you let it drive you to success.

ADDITIONAL LESSONS

Good Customer Service Builds Trust
A gentle answer turns away wrath, but a harsh word stirs up anger. This statement addresses the idea of good customer service. A wise heart shows understanding and sweet and kind speech can be very persuasive. Thus selling is about turning an opportunity into a sale. It is the art of convincing with honesty, understanding, reasoning and answering questions. This statement underscores the importance of advertising and marketing your business. One of the best marketing tools is good customer service, and that means treating your customers respectfully and fairly. Even when it appears that your marketing efforts are not paying off, it is important not to be discouraged and keep at it until you find success.

Building trust in business is critical. When it comes to service, trust that has been established is what leads to a sale. Furthermore, it is important to remember to pay attention to our customers; try to satisfy and meet their needs.

The Second Knot and Making a Profit
The art of negotiation is a much needed skill as it relates to being successful in business. The buyer wants something they need and could not get by themselves. The seller has what the buyer needs and sells it for a profit. At the end of the business transaction, there will be mutual benefit for both the seller and the buyer.

Another key ingredient to good negotiation outcomes is to ensure that you price your goods or services correctly. A winning price attracts a willing customer; whereas a losing price will drive the customer away. The individual who possesses wisdom always has the advantage of gaining success as it relates to business. Focus and specializing in a message, product, or service is a prudent and wise ingredient to being successful in business.

The Third Knot & Household Needs
Profits sustain the business and provides for basic needs. The idea of trying to get rich quick is a recipe for disaster and the temptation should be avoided. Many people want a business; however they talk a lot and work not at all and time passes with nothing ever getting done. The motto, "Less talk and more action," both in business as well as life, is a recipe for good success. The old idiom, "Slow and steady wins the race," illustrates that in business, one must learn to pace progress, avoid get rich quick offers, and work with diligence.

ADDITIONAL LESSONS

Trading Without Money
Long before the idea or invention of currency, people used bartering as a means of getting required goods and services. In Africa, though not as common as in years past, people still exchange goods and services via bartering. In fact, you have probably bartered yourself. Have you ever traded your snack for your friends drink? That's a form of bartering!

Teaching Others
It is important to share information, knowledge and things that will benefit others. Give things to others freely and share ideas, processes, strategies, possessions and it will come back to bless you. In this story, Okon and Nkoyo learned about business from their Aunt Gloria Ekong. They willing shared what they had learned with their best friends Daraima and Edidoing. There is a common proverbial statement that states that a generous person will be prosperous, and the person who gives will also be given.

Cleaning Up and Closing Down
Learning when to stop work is important otherwise there is the possibility of becoming a workaholic. Closing business for the day prepares the body for rest and relaxation. It should be that a person who works hard should always reap the benefits of their labor. It is wise to slow down at the end of the day, so we can continue to be effective and productive the following day.

The Fourth Knot, Good Helpers & the Reward
The idea of being successful in business is attainable with the right team of people, and based on loyal people who can work for you diligently. In addition, the fourth knot represents leisure spending and rewarding yourself and your significant others for a hard job well done.

Hard Work Always Pays Off
Satisfaction in one's work is one of the greatest accomplishments in life. Too many people seek more success, more money, and more awards instead of enjoying the fruit of their labor. Take a moment to stop, and enjoy the benefits of working hard. Conversely, the lazy businessman will get what he gives: nothing.

Reflection & Rest
As we obtain our money and build worth it is important to know what we are to do with it.

ADDITIONAL LESSONS

The Fifth Knot & Doing Important Things of Interest
Money has always been obtained to do something. Money should not be obtained to be greedy; neither should money be hoarded or spent carelessly. However, money should be spent on meaningful endeavors that benefit our immediate communities, the world and important causes. Also, it is wise not to turn a blind eye to those in need.

References:
NewFangled Web Factory from Web Smart Newsletter:
Proverbs and Ecclesiastes on Business
originally published February 2005 - Updated July 2006 by Eric Holter.
http://www.newfangled.com/the_nature_of_business
Business and the Bible by Lara Velez of Moms of Faith www.momsoffaith.com, and Rachel Lower of Christian Mommies
www.christian-mommies.com

ADDITIONAL LESSONS

Meaning of Efik/Ibibio Names:
Abasi-Oku – Joy from the heart or sweetheart (unisex name)
Ambo – The name of Efik clan
Archibong – A person who crowns or anoints a king or a king maker
Bassey – god
Ekong – War
Eno-Obong – The gift of God
Daraima – Celebrate Love (male name)
Edidoing – Blessing (unisex name)
Effiong – A person who is born on a market day
Ekanem – Source
Essien – Outside or Belongs to everyone (male name)
Eteka – Grandpa or name after grandfather
Inyang – Sea
Nkoyo – Queen (female name)
Obong – God or Lord (unisex name)
Okon – Born at night (male name)

Nigerian Names:
Jide – Hold tight
Kunle – Arrived home
Nzelibe – A king that has taken shelter
Tunde – My Father has arrived again or father returns (Tunde is a short variation for Babatunde)
Uchechukwu – The heart or mind of God
Uzoho – New road or What a road

QUESTIONS:

MENTAL & PENCIL ACTIVITIES

Money Belt Knots

Put the correct letter in each of the 5 knots. Then write examples of each under the knot. One example has been started for you.

A. Pay for house

A. Household needs
B. Future Projects
C. Luxuries, rewards and charity
D. Profit
E. Breaking Even

Matching: Business Terminology

Draw a line connecting each description to the word it correctly represents or means.

| Trading goods and/or services without money | 1. Commerce |

| The extra money made after all expenses are paid | 2. Profit |

| Business; making money | 3. Reward |

| When you receive all money put into the business | 4. Goal |

| Incentive; prize; compensation | 5. Bartering |

| Something you want to accomplish or achieve | 6. Breaking Even |

Nigerian Terminology Crossword puzzle

1. A tropical fruit that looks like a banana, but can be cooked like a potato
2. A mat woven together like basket
3. A cash register worn around the waist
4. An Efik King
5. A tropical flu-like illness commonly transmitted by mosquitoes; it can be fatal for the unhealthy and malnourished
6. Nigerian money and currency used for the exchange of goods and services

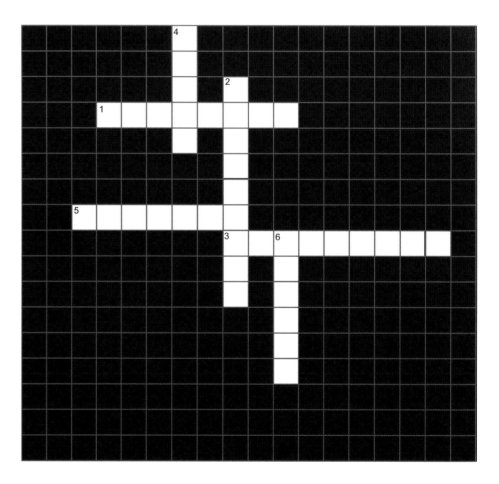

Goal Setting

1. What do you like to do? What do you want to be when you grow up?

_____

2. People often set goals to lose weight, make good grades, save money (for a bike, toy, car or house), or do something for the first time (e.g., invent something, be the first in their family to go to college, etc).
   a. What are some things you would like to do in school?

_____

   b. This summer?

_____

   c. Five years from now?

_____

   d. What can you do to achieve these goals?

_____

3. Put an X over the one thing that will not help you achieve your goals.
a. Child spending all money on candy or other nonsense | b. Child studying | c. Youth working and getting paid

4. Write down your goal, share it with a parent or friend who will encourage you to work hard.

_____

_____

ADDITIONAL LESSONS

Rational

The New African School was written to reinforce the concept of the educational experience and to underscore the importance of academics, order, respect, camaraderie, healthy competition, encouragement, and how school shapes our future.

Walking Back from School

As kids growing up, we heard stories from our parents about their walking several miles to school. In some instances, there were chores to be done before going to school such as fetching water. Hearing these stories brought a realization that there was struggle or difficulties that were faced, and only those determined or strong willed would make it. Walking can be relaxing and keeps the body physically fit. Walking offers a time of meditation and quiet reflection when alone, but it can offer some time for great bonding between friends.

A Study Plan

Studying for exams can be tedious, but sometimes the competitive side of us can foster a positive aspect that propels us forward to succeed. The key to life is to develop a strategy, a game plan and to follow this plan with some degree of flexibility. A Chemistry professor in college once told us on a Friday afternoon "out of nothing comes nothing". This was said in the context that if you don't study you will not get anything and that you must put forward an effort to study so as to excel academically. It does no good to cram for a test the night before, study hours, days and even weeks before so that it becomes part of you and it becomes a lesson you learn for life and not just for an exam.

National Common Entrance Examination

Many people dread tests and exams. In fact many sometimes start feeling sick, tired or bored just thinking about the exam and the possible outcome of an exam. It is important to note that your knowledge or skill in an area cannot be measured if an exam or test is not given. Testing should be regarded as fun and the way to overcome the ills of it is to look forward to the results and the benefits of passing it.

School Visits and Interviews

It is always a good idea to go and see what you are chasing or seeking and desiring. Sometimes what you think you want or feel is good for you may in fact not be.

ADDITIONAL LESSONS

Interviewing offers an opportunity to see and learn things that are not always obvious or apparent. Being asked questions or asking the questions can help you get your bearings, evaluate and confirm if your heart really wants what you have been pursing.

Touch Down
Sometimes you will have to leave where you are or where you are comfortable to gain perspective. Perspective is always advantageous in ultimately making the right decision.

Interviewing with the Best
Okon learned that Kaduna was where he wanted to go to school. However, his exam results took him in another direction that did not seem to give him his first choice. The good news is that he had a second option or what some call a plan B and it was plan B that paved the way for his bright future. Additionally, it was a good thing and very fortunate that Okon was able to cultivate the attitude of being flexible and this contributed to his being able to adjust quickly and succeed.

Try Your Best and Don't Give Up
There is an old idiom that states "if at first you don't succeed then try and try again." Often times trying again will offer a degree of success that one desires. However, it must be stated and underscored that one should know when ones efforts are not reaping any rewards and another path must be set that should be pursued.

School Starts
There is always a lot to do in terms of preparation before anything starts and this could not be truer as it relates to starting school. Okon found out that he had no time to cry over spilled milk, and had to get himself focused for school.

The First Day of Boarding School
The first time doing something or going somewhere new can be very exciting. On the other hand, there could also be the emotion of fear. Irrespective of the emotion there will come a point when the experience which was new becomes old. During the new stages it is important to have the right advice and proper encouragement. Fortunately, for Okon his wise and caring uncle filled in for his father and his mother also filled in as an excellent support system.

ADDITIONAL LESSONS

Are We There Yet

We should learn to control or temper some of our emotions and being anxious is one of them. Anxiety stems from being impatient and this can oftentimes cause unnecessary stress. All things being equal we will get to the anticipated destination or occasion, but in the meantime we should exercise self control. In the process of exercising patience we learn or even see things that are new that we may not have noticed or overlooked. What we observe or learn may in fact come in handy for another occasion so it is important not to be anxious for anything.

A Goodbye Tear

Boarding school is an experience that really forges an individual and can make them very strong. Boys generally assume that crying is a sign of weakness, but it is a way to release the pressure value of emotion that is building up. A good cry frees the system and allows the healing process to begin. Obviously, Okon missed his loved ones and so did some of the other kids and this is normal and should be expected.

On Your Own

There are many things in life that you will have to face by yourself. Doing things for oneself is a pivotal part of growing up and is a sign of independence. It is important to note that no matter how independent we become we will always need someone or something at some point or another. Our parents should always be there for us and may be wise instruments of counsel in the years to come.

The Meeting

Meetings are always a great forum to learn and to have information clarified. Some meetings can be long and seem boring or never ending. However, it is important to learn to gather the necessary information from meetings as they may prove to be very beneficial. Meetings also serve to smooth out any bumps or misunderstandings that may arise or have already arisen.

Staying Focused

Focus is required for a number of things and it is very important to be focused when in school. In Africa and many continents of the world academics is the ticket to a number of opportunities and for doors to open. These days, it is more challenging to not be impacted by negative peer pressures, but it is with focus a singleness of vision and attitude that these temptations can be overcome. In

ADDITIONAL LESSONS

addition to staying focused it is essential to stay organized. Organization helps streamline tasks and helps keep the right attention on items that need to be taken care of with more ease.

Lights Out
Everything must come to an end and this is very much so as it relates to our day to day activities. In reality, lights out really is a temporary stop to all active activity except for those that sustain life. Before lights are turned out it offers the student an opportunity to tie up any loose ends, and then it offers an opportunity for reflection of the day. This may be the time to think about how to improve on the faults of the day and make a commitment to make the next one a better one.

The Wake-Up Call
The wake-up call is so critical to ensure that the day starts off on time. We are the ones who are supposed to be in control of our attitude, and it is our choice to make it positive and ensure that the external forces that try to make it negative do not prevail. Starting things on time is energizing and it allows us to stay on course or on task. To wake up is another opportunity to try to make the day better than the one before by learning from past errors and committing to improve previous successes.

Monday Morning School Assembly
Assembly is part of the communal as well as relational aspects of our human experience. Assembly especially in a school setting can reaffirm values and clarify things that are ongoing or planned in the future. This was Okon's first assembly at his new school and it was a moment that strengthened his resolve to do his best.

What's in You Will Help You
Whether it is assembly or some other occasion, a person, a belief or an item that strengthens our determination; it is important that it lasts and carries us for a longtime until we see the benefits of such an effort. In Okon's case it was the deposit and the contributions that were made by his family that shaped him. In fact, this solid foundation that was laid was what he drew from to help him succeed. For many of us this is true and even more importantly is the spiritual aspects of our being that bring balance as well as success in the serious game of life.

QUESTIONS

1. What sounds filled the air around Mrs. Gloria Ekong's house?

2. When did Mrs. Ekong's day begin?

3. What was Mrs. Ekong's husband's name?

4. What day did Mrs. Ekong plan to go to the market?

5. What did Mrs. Ekong put on after getting dressed?

6. Who came knocking on Mrs. Ekong's door?

7. What did Okon and Nkoyo eat before going to the market with their aunty?

8. What famous palace did Mrs. Ekong, Okon and Nkoyo pass in Calabar on their way to the market?

9. What is commerce?

10. What amazed Okon and Nkoyo as they walked down the streets of the market place?

11. What was Mrs. Gloria Ekong's shop number?

12. What was the number of the shop next door and who owned it?

13. What was Mrs. Ekong doing as the kids where catching their breath?

14. What items were cut into smaller bunches and placed on raffia mats?

15. A woman with a baby on her back came into the store and bought which items?

16. How much change did Mrs. Ekong give back to the woman with the baby on her back?

17. Who noticed that their aunt had tied off a knot in her money belt?

18. In business according to Mrs. Ekong the first goal should be to do this?

19. What is profit?

20. Which items did Mr. Essien buy in Mrs. Mary Archibong's shop?

21. Why had Mrs. Ekong not seen Mr. Essien for a long time?

22. How old was Akwa, Mr. Essien's daughter about turn?

23. The children had noticed a second knot in their aunt's money belt, what was the meaning of this knot?

24. After lunch the shop had sold most of these items?

25. Why was Nkoyo leaping for joy?

26. What did the third knot in Mrs. Gloria Ekong's money belt mean?

27. What does it mean to barter according to Mrs. Ekong?

28. What did Mrs. Ekong barter with Mrs. Archibong?

29. Daraima was whose best friend?

30. What grade level was Edidiong?

31. Besides breaking even, profits and what to do with profit what else did Okon and Nkoyo share with Daraima and Edidiong about business?

32. The children were feeling a little rushed and planned to meet here during the week to talk more about business?

33. As they clean the shop to close for the day, Nkoyo was asked to do this as part of her activities to close the shop?

34. What was Okon asked to do as part of his activities to close the shop?

35. The kids had worked very hard all day and their aunty decided to give this to them?

36. What could a reward do?

37. From where did Mrs. Gloria Ekong take out the reward money?

38. What does money in the fourth knot mean?

39. What did the kids do with their reward money?

40. Who asked about the possibility of a fifth knot and what could this money be used for?

QUESTIONS

A. Why did Okon choose to walk home from school rather than fix his bike?

B. Interview your parents and grandparents.

Ask them the following questions:

a. How did you get to school every day?

b. How far away was school from your house?

c. What was your school schedule like?

d. What responsibilities did you have before and/or after school?

C. In Nigeria, students go off to boarding school around the age of 11. Would you like to go to boarding school? Why or why not?

D. In the Nigerian grading system, everyone's names and grades are posted for every assignment and exam. How is the Nigerian grading system different than the system in your school? List at least three good and bad things about each system.

E. Since Okon's family advocated good grades and hard work, he knew he would do well in school. What are some things your family values that will help you do well in school and life?

F. Explain the purpose/significance of a) the educational system, b) religion, and c) physical health in terms of becoming a well rounded person? Should b & c be a part of educational training? Why or why not?

G. The campus design (e.g., building appearances & layout, amenities) and upkeep (e.g., unkempt vs. manicured lawns) communicate organizational values, financial conditions and ambiance to students, staff and visitors. Draw a picture of FSG: Enugu, your own school or your ideal school grounds. Explain the impression you want to convey to visitors, staff or students and how the choices of materials, aesthetics, etc. enable you to do this.

FILL IN THE BLANK:

Fill in the blanks with the words in the box.

Ibo	Class One	Harmattan	Boarding School	Hausa	prefect

Mrs. Musa was from the _____ tribe. Her tribe lives in northern Nigeria and is usually Muslim. She did not like _____ because it is the Nigerian equivalent of winter—though it doesn't get cooler than 60°F.

Okon is _____. His tribe lives in eastern Nigeria and is known for being hard working. He was preparing to go to _____ _____ where he would study, live, and eat until he graduated.

Okon was a _____ _____ or first year student, who was supposed to obey the students in the grades above his. In particular, he was to respect the disciplinary authority of the class _____ students.

THE AFRICAN SCHOOL

Here are some important lessons you can learn from this story. Explain why each of these is important. OR List examples of each of these in the story. OR List some important lessons/values in your family and how these have helped you OR why they are important.

A.) **A good name/do not shame your family**

B.) **Work hard**

C.) **Delayed gratification**

D.) **Working for what you want instead of being given everything**

E.) **Making friends**

F.) **Respecting your elders**

G.) **Good stewardship/watch your yam**

ADDITIONAL QUESTIONS

1. How far was the walk home from school?
2. How many students were at St. Silas Primary School?
3. Why did Okon not want to spend his money to fix his bike's tire?
4. What was it that Okon's father told him would end up not being valued as much?
5. Okon's friend Rotimi Johnson was good in these subjects?
6. What subjects was Okon good at in school?
7. Who was Okon going to visit during the summer holiday?
8. How many daily hours did Okon and Rotimi study for their exams?
9. Why did Okon and Rotimi cut back on their daily study hours?
10. Who honked her horn to take Rotimi and Okon to the examination center?
11. What was it that Okon was expecting to arrive?
12. What else came with the mail that Okon was expecting?
13. What was the name of the pilot for the flight Okon took from Calabar to Kaduna?
14. How high was the plane flying from Calabar to Kaduna?
15. Why was Mrs. Musa wearing a white scarf to protect her face?
16. Why did Mrs. Musa hate the harmattan?
17. What experience had Mrs. Musa suffered the previous year because of harmattan?
18. Which school had Okon been accepted to based on his performance on his common entrance exams?
19. Was Okon pleased that he was accepted to this school?
20. Who did Okon meet with at Federal Government College Kaduna to see if he could be accepted to the school?
21. Why did Okon have to leave his aunty and Kaduna?
22. What did Pastor Sunday Adeboye do for Okon?
23. Who came to take Okon to his new school and give him fatherly advice?
24. Mr. James Bassey was doing this during the time Okon was heading off to school?
25. What additional advice did Mr. Inyang give Okon?
26. What is the meaning of the African Proverb "a poor man's yam never gets burnt"?
27. This was the school motto shown at the entrance of Federal Government College Enugu?
28. Name the five dormitories at Federal Government College Enugu?
29. Okon did this as his mother and uncle drove out of the school car park?
30. Who was one of the entry students Okon meet?
31. What made this entry student unusual?
32. Which article of clothing easily identified senior students?
33. Were prefects respected and what did they do?
34. What did Okon do after the mandatory meeting that introduced the head boy and the prefects?
35. This happened at 7:00AM?
36. This happened on most nights at 7:00PM?
37. How many other students shared the dorm room with Okon?
38. When was visiting Sunday?
39. What were the rumors about the Assistant Head Master, Mr. Tunde Bakere?
40. Why was Okon happy at assembly?
41. Hearing about coming first in class caused Okon to do this?
42. What did Okon Bassey come to understand about the grading system?
43. Okon Bassey's upbringing was going to do this and why was this?
44. What did Okon make up his mind to do?
45. Okon shouted this as he collected his books from his school locker to go back to the dormitory?

ANSWERS

1. The air was already filling with the sounds of cars and buses passing by on their way to work, the clattering of pots and pans that would be used to prepare a morning meal. If you listened closely you could even hear the sounds of porches and the yard being swept with brushes made from palm fronds.
2. Mrs. Gloria Ekong's day started early before the roaster crowed
3. Eno-Obong Ekong
4. Saturday, Ambo Market day
5. She put on her money belt
6. Mrs. Ekong's nephew Okon, and her niece Nkoyo had been dropped off by her sister Margaret
7. They ate a quick breakfast of bean cakes, eggs, sweet bread and orange juice.
8. They passed the famous palace of Obong Ekpe Bassey of Calabar
9. Commerce is the art and action of making money by selling goods or services.
10. The children were both amazed at how busy everyone seemed as they walked down the streets of the market place
11. Her shop number was 333
12. The shop next door was number 334 and it was owned by Mrs. Mary Archibong.
13. Mrs. Ekong began washing and arranging her fruits and vegetables
14. Bananas and plantains
15. The woman with the baby bought two dozen tomatoes, ten onions, twenty peppers and forty okra pods.

16. She gave her back two naira
17. Okon noticed that she had tied off a knot in her money belt
18. In business, one of your first goals should be to recover the money you started the business with, and this is called 'breaking even'
19. Profit is the extra money that is made after breaking even
20. Mr. Essien had bought peanuts and yams from Mrs. Archibong
21. Mr. Essien had been sick with malaria
22. Akwa was about to celebrate her sixth birthday
23. The second knot meant that their aunt had made a profit
24. After lunch the shop had sold most of the vegetables
25. Nkoyo was leaping for joy because she had noticed a third knot in her aunt's money belt.
26. The third knot in Mrs. Gloria Ekong's money belt meant she had made enough money to take care of all of her household needs
27. To barter is to exchange goods and services without paying for it with money
28. Mrs. Ekong bartered okra, oranges and plantains worth thirty naira for omo clothing washing detergent and soap also worth thirty naira with Mrs. Archibong
29. Daraima was Okon's best friend
30. Edidiong was in primary two
31. Daraima and Edidiong learned how to treat customers
32. The children planned to meet on their school play ground during the week to talk more about business
33. Nkoyo was asked by her aunty to get the broom and sweep the entire shop

THE AFRICAN MARKET WOMAN

ANSWERS & PUZZLE WORD ANSWERS

34. Okon was instructed to start taking down the stacks of oranges, tomatoes, pepper and onions that were not sold and place them in the bags that were used to bring them into the shop earlier that morning

35. Mrs. Gloria Ekong gave Okon and Nkoyo a reward of five naira each

36. A reward gives the person receiving it something to look forward to and a reason to work towards something

37. She took it out of a fourth knot that was in her money belt

38. The fourth knot holds money that Mrs. Ekong uses to spend on things she wants such as fixing her hair, shopping for a dress or shoes, buying a gift for a friend, giving money to the poor and needy, and rewarding hard working nieces and nephews for helping her at the store

39. The kids spent some of their reward money on candy.

40. Nkoyo asked about the possibility of a fifth knot which could be used to build and fund other things one is interested in

PUZZLE WORD ANSWERS:

1. Plantain
2. Raffia Mat
3. Money Belt
4. Obong
5. Malaria
6. Naira

ANSWERS

1. The walk home from school was three miles long.
2. St. Silas Primary School had over six hundred students.
3. Okon did not want to spend his money because he was saving it for the national common entrance examination fees.
4. Okon's father told him that whatever you get easily and without effort you end up not valuing as much.
5. Rotimi Johnson was good at math and science.
6. Okon was good in English language, social studies and literature.
7. Okon was going to visit Mrs. Musa his mother's good friend in Kaduna.
8. They studied for three hours a day.
9. They cut back their study hours because Okon had not been getting enough rest, and his mother asked him to cut his study down to 2 hours a day.
10. Rotimi's mother took Rotimi and Okon to the exam.
11. Okon was expecting his plane ticket from Mrs. Musa for his trip to Kaduna.
12. The mail also contained a prospective letter from Federal Government College Kaduna.
13. The name of the pilot was Captain John Obianyor.
14. The plane was flying at an altitude of thirty six thousand feet.
15. Mrs. Musa was wearing a scarf to protect her face from the cold harmattan weather.
16. Mrs. Musa hated the harmattan's cold conditions.
17. Mrs. Musa had suffered feverish conditions and catarrh the previous year because of the harmattan.
18. Okon had been accepted to Federal Government College Enugu his second choice pick.
19. No, Okon was disappointed that he got into this school as he wanted to stay with his aunty and attend Federal Government College Kaduna.
20. Okon met with the headmaster of the school Mr. Kunle Coker.
21. Okon had to leave Kaduna so he could return home to Calabar to begin preparing for school in Enugu.
22. Pastor Sunday Adeboye prayed for Okon. Also, he advised Okon to pursue excellence in everything, to strive to be a leader, and to make a positive effort in the right direction with his studies.
23. Okon's uncle, Mr. Victor Inyang came to take him to his new school and give him fatherly advice.
24. Mr. James Bassey had traveled out of the country for a very important medical conference in which he was a speaker.
25. Mr. Inyang advised Okon to be obedient to his teachers and seniors, and to make the family proud.
26. A rich man has many yams, so he can afford to play around while his yams are in the fire. However, if any of his yams get burnt he simply gets more yams to replace it. On the other hand, a poor man has only one yam. This one yam is all he has and is forced to watch it with care while it roasts in the fire.
27. The school motto was unity and peace.
28. Peace House, Liberty House, Unity House, Honesty House, and Independence House
29. Okon began to cry as he waved goodbye to his family.

ANSWERS

30. One of the entry students Okon met Jide Nzelibe.

31. Jide was unusual as he was born in the United States of America in the city of Cleveland in the state of Ohio. Also, Jide's mother was an American.

32. Senior students were easily identified because they wore trousers instead of shorts.

33. Yes, prefects were respected because of the authority they had been given, and they were responsible for managing their various areas.

34. Okon went back to his room, and continued to read the student's handbook.

35. Morning Inspection

36. Evening Prep

37. Nine other students shared the dorm room with Okon

38. Visiting Sunday was the last Sunday of the month.

39. The rumor about Mr. Tunde Bakere was that he did not tolerate nonsense, and getting into trouble with him was to be avoided at all costs.

40. Okon was happy at assembly because he liked the headmaster's comments, and because he got to meet with this new classmates.

41. Hearing about coming first in class caused Okon to remember what his uncle had told him in the car "Okon do not shame us, do your best, and make us proud."

42. Okon Bassey came to understand that the grading system created an environment of fierce competition among the student.

43. Okon's upbringing was going to pay off, because his family had already laid a good foundation for both academics and hard work.

44. Okon made up his mind that he was going to shine like a star, and excel beyond anyone's expectations including his.

45. Okon shouted "The fight is on and the game begins."

MAP OF AFRICA

ATLANTIC

OCEAN

FLAGS OF AFRICAN COUNTRIES

 Algeria

 Angola

 Benin

 Botswana

 Burkina Faso

 Burundi

 Cameroon

Cape Verde

 Central African R.

 Chad

 Congo

 Côte d'Ivoire

 Djibouti

 Egypt

 Equatorial Guinea

 Eritrea

 Ethiopia

 Gabon

 Ghana

 Guinea-Bissau

 Guinea

 Kenya

 Lesotho

Liberia

 Libya

 Madagascar

 Malawi

 Mali

 Mauritania

 Morocco

 Mozambique

Namibia

 Niger

 Nigeria

 Republic of Congo

 Rwanda

 Senegal

 Seychelles

 Sierra Leone

Somalia

 South Africa

 Sudan

 Swaziland

 Tanzania

 The Gambia

 Togo

 Tunisia

 Uganda

 Zambia

 Zimbabwe

AUTHORS' REMARKS

The world media has successfully branded Africa as the "dark continent". If it's bad, it is Africa. From civil wars, to droughts which bring about starvation, to diseases like AIDS and malaria, to corruption in government, and the list goes on. Needless to say, if you were to ask the average person what they thought of when you say the word Africa, most responses would not be gold, oil, and precious stones. They may say it is a continent of beautiful skies, lush lands, thick forests, cool mountains, rich grasslands, wide jungles, fresh rivers and even arid deserts with unique forms of life. Irrespective of your view or what you think out loud, when it is all said and done Africa is good!

Africa's greatest asset is its people; people of different hues and very diverse backgrounds. Africa's people are defined by their faith in God and a rich cultural heritage. At the center of African culture are its values. Values are transferred via stories and experiences. African values honor and cherish the elderly, and celebrate new life with great fervor. Africa respects its women and elevates its men. Values are what defines and makes Africa standout. Values are in abundance in Africa. Africa is willing to express, share and pass on her values and this is in part what makes Africa good!

Africa is looked upon as a beggar continent to be helped by others who are not African. Growing-up the simple question that always came to mind was "can anything good come out of Africa?" Somewhere and somehow it has been mysteriously embedded in the minds of most Africans that Africa has nothing good. All the good things came from overseas; from Italian shoes to German and Japanese cars to everything that has a made in America tag.

Africans are glued to American television and thereby imbibe the American 'good' values to replace the bad African values.

Before continuing, we must say that our objective is not to put down other cultures. However, our objective is to show the world and to remind Africans that we indeed have many good things to be thankful for. Did you know that the most educated sub-group in America is West Africans? Many of our secondary school classmates are now doctors, lawyers, and in other prominent professions living all over world; they have attested to the fact that the values of hard work, a strong extended family unit, a good educational system, grounded in unyielding faith they received from Africa is what made the difference in their achievements. Again, all of this infuses and reinforces the idea that Africa is good!

There is a theory that states that whatever is focused upon will expand. We have chosen and want to focus on the good of Africa, and would like to invite you to foster that expansion so as to overwhelm the bad.

Lawrence Nyong & Obi Chidebelu-Eze
Authors

ACKNOWLEDGMENTS

Tiffani Adomey

Samantha Angeli

Tressie Anigbo

Sylvester Anigbo

Carlton Arthurs

Fiona Arthurs

Paul Arthurs

Sheila Arthurs

Dr. Dale C. Bronner

Andrea P. F. Brooks

Kunle Coker

Chioma Chidebelu-Eze

Chukwuemeka Chidebelu-Eze

Jonathan Chidebelu-Eze

Jordyn Chidebelu-Eze

Maduka Chidebelu-Eze

Mia Chidebelu-Eze

Sarah Chidebelu-Eze

Taryn Chidebelu-Eze

Roselyn Daniels

Dr. Caroline C. Eze

Dr. Ezekiel Guti

Georgina Garrick

Tim Krahenbuhl

Gail Krahenbuhl

Derrick Jackson

Patrice Jackson

Josh Murtha

David Newborne

Cynthia Newborne

Bassey Nyong

David Nyong

Effiong Nyong

Eliane Nyong

Emmanuel Nyong

Essien Nyong

Faith Nyong

Gloria Nyong

Ifeoma Nyong

Joseph Nyong

Lauren Nyong

Lawrence Nyong

Victor Nyong

Jide Nzelibe

Edidem Ekpo Okon Abasi Otu V

Dominique Stewart

James Ward

Sharon Ward

P. Buxton Williams

Former Ambassador Andrew Young

AUTHORS' AND ILLUSTRATOR'S BIOS

Lawrence Nyong was born in Calabar, Nigeria. He immigrated to the United States, and attended Oral Roberts University where he graduated in 1995 with a business degree. Upon graduating, he found employment in Chicago, Illinois with K-mart where he began his working career as a manager. In 1997, Lawrence joined Sherwin Williams Paint Company based in Cleveland Ohio. As a sales and marketing representative with the consumer group division of the company, he covered Illinois, Indiana and the Wisconsin markets.

community with mentoring programs, leading business camps and sharing wisdom via children's books. In addition, he is on a mission to change the perception of Africa from the inside out. Lawrence has coined the phrase, "you can go anywhere from anywhere, all you need to do is decide where you want to go."

Lawrence lives in Chicago, Illinois with his wife, Faith and his three gifted children, Lawrence II, Lauren and Victor.

After nine years of corporate work, he decided to take an early retirement to grow his own business in 2006. Lawrence is a gifted entrepreneur and has started several companies over the years. He is sort after for business related advice and is always willing to help others and to see them succeed. In addition to overseeing his companies, he sits on the board of several companies and non-profit organizations.

Lawrence is passionate about educating and preparing the youth for the future. He believes that it is critical that youth are equipped to assume roles as responsible and productive citizens. To this end, he is active in his

AUTHORS' AND ILLUSTRATOR'S BIOS

Obi Chidebelu-Eze was born in Enugu, Nigeria and came to the USA in 1989. He holds a Bachelor of Science degree from Oral Roberts University in Biology and a MBA in Marketing from the University of Phoenix. In 2008, Obi decided to pursue his passion of writing and publishing full time via his own company. Consequently, leaving Kimberly-Clark Corporation in Roswell, Georgia where he had been employed as a scientist and business analyst for ten years. Obi is also an educator and spends much of his time teaching children science at the middle school level.

Obi lives in Atlanta, Georgia with his wonderful wife, Mia, and their two gifted children Jonathan and Jordyn.

In 1999, Obi started Dove Publishing, Inc. primarily to showcase his creative gift of writing and painting. In addition to The Tales of Tortoise published in 2005, The Lion That Finally Roared published in 2008, and Africa Is Good 1 & 2 published in 2011. Obi has written several other original short children's stories which also have fun teachings. These unpublished stories include: The Healing Pot, Princess Chinyere, Wisdom and The Bird that Talked and he is currently working on a few other book related manuscripts and projects. These stories are geared to teach children sound and moral values, and emphasize specific topics that are subtitled in each book. Obi strongly believes that children are the future and every effort to invest in their proper development is the direction we all must take.

AUTHORS' AND ILLUSTRATOR'S BIOS

David F. Newborne was born in Nashville, and, while an infant, moved with his parents, David and Julia Newborne to Memphis.

As a young child, David was exposed to the arts through the city's rich musical heritage and his very musical family. His father was a high school band director. His mother sang and played piano in the church.

David's interest and participation in music branched off into visual art and design, enabling him to win numerous art contests while in school. This led to his decision to attend Tennessee State University in Nashville where he majored in architectural engineering. There, he played trumpet with the marching band and designed the band uniforms and school logos.

He is a multi-faceted artistic designer and illustrator. The talents that God has placed in him to bring pictorial life to writers' words are evident in this book, The Tales of Tortoise, The Lion That Finally Roared and others, such as The Lady King and With Unveiled Faces.

David now resides in Atlanta, Georgia with his wife Cynthia, his greatest inspiration. They are the proud parents of Tiffani, Taryn, David Troy and Traci, all of whom are gifted. He also has five grandsons Joshua, Jonas, Gabriel, Luke and Mark.